Andy Shane

and the

Pumpkin Trick

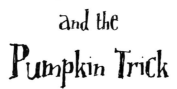

Andy Shane
and the
Pumpkin Trick

Jennifer Richard Jacobson

illustrated by Abby Carter

CANDLEWICK PRESS
CAMBRIDGE, MASSACHUSETTS

In memory of Sam and Eva Holder
J. R. J.

For Leah, Lauren, and Jamie
A. C.

Text copyright © 2006 by Jennifer Richard Jacobson
Illustrations copyright © 2006 by Abby Carter

All rights reserved. No part of this book may be reproduced, transmitted,or stored
in an information retrieval system in any form or by any means, graphic, electronic,
or mechanical, including photocopying, taping, and recording, without prior
written permission from the publisher.

First edition 2006

Library of Congress Cataloging-in-Publication Data

Jacobson, Jennifer, date.
Andy Shane and the pumpkin trick / Jennifer Richard Jacobson ;
illustrated by Abby Carter. —1st ed.
p.   cm.
Summary: Andy Shane, with help from Grandma Webb
and some marbles, tricks the people who keep stealing his friend
Dolores Starbuckle's Halloween pumpkins.
ISBN 0-7636-2605-8
[1. Pumpkin—Fiction. 2. Halloween—Fiction. 3. Grandmothers—Fiction.
4. Marbles (Game objects)—Fiction.]
I. Carter, Abby, ill. II. Title.
PZ7.J1529Al 2006
[E]—dc22   2004062872

2 4 6 8 10 9 7 5 3 1

Printed in the United States of America

This book was typeset in Vendome.
The illustrations were done in black pencil and black watercolor wash.

Candlewick Press
2067 Massachusetts Avenue
Cambridge, Massachusetts 02140

visit us at www.candlewick.com

CONTENTS

1
Trapped

"So, Andy Shane," said Granny Webb, "which pumpkin shall we choose for our jack-o'-lantern this year?"

Andy stepped back to take a good look at the pumpkins he and Granny had grown. Should he pick a big, fat, round pumpkin? Or a tall, skinny pumpkin? They all seemed to say, "Pick me! Pick me!"

"Helloooooo there!" shouted a
voice.

Granny Webb and Andy Shane
looked up.

Dolores Starbuckle was walking
down the path, waving a white
envelope in her hand.

Andy dived onto his belly between
rows of pumpkins.

Granny laughed. "Too late, Andy
Shane. You've definitely been
spotted."

"Andy Shane," called Dolores as
she approached, "you forgot your
invitation at school."

Dolores's birthday was in two
days. So was Halloween.

"I wouldn't want you to forget my party," said Dolores. "And I know that you'll need time to think about my present."

"Oh, we wouldn't have forgotten," said Granny Webb. "I promised your mother I would help out this year."

Andy looked up at Granny Webb. How could she? Now he was really trapped into going.

"Wow!" exclaimed Dolores. "Did you and Granny grow all these pumpkins, Andy Shane?"

"Yup," Andy said. "We sure did!"

"You're lucky," said Dolores. "We bought a pumpkin at Glories of Nature, but someone came along and smashed it last night."

"Someone smashed your pumpkin?" asked Andy. "Why would they do that?"

Granny Webb shook her head. "Such a waste. Come inside, Dolores, and help us make pumpkin muffins for your birthday. Then you can tell us all about those tricksters."

The minute Dolores entered Andy's house, she began poking around. She picked up a jar of marbles from the kitchen counter.

"Whose are these?" she asked.

"Mine," said Andy.

"I like the big marble at the bottom. Ooooh, and look at this sparkly one here!" said Dolores. "Will you play marbles with me sometime?"

Andy didn't know what to say.

"Tell us more about the tricksters," said Granny, mixing up the muffin batter.

"As soon as it got dark, they smashed all the pumpkins on our street," said Dolores.

"Did anyone catch them?" asked Andy.

"Nope," said Dolores. "No one heard them."

"We'll have to give you another pumpkin, then," said Granny Webb.

When they returned to the
pumpkin patch, Dolores charged
over to the biggest, fattest one.

"Isn't this the best pumpkin?"
said Dolores as she picked it from
the vine.

It *did* seem to be the best one. But then Andy noticed a rounder, jollier pumpkin, and another that was more orange than the rest. *They're ALL the best,* he thought.

"Great," said Granny Webb. "As soon as the muffins are done, I'll drive you and your pumpkin home."

"Can Andy come, too?"

"Sure," said Granny Webb.

"He can stay and help me get ready for my party," said Dolores.

"Get ready for your party?" said

Andy. "It's two days away!"

"It's never too early to prepare for

a social event," noted Dolores.

2
Party Plans

Dolores carried the pumpkin from Granny's truck to her front porch. She put it on the left side of the steps.

"We need to find its best side,"

Dolores said.

She turned the pumpkin around

and around.

"Perfect!" she said finally. "Let's get ready for the party!"

Andy made a face. He was definitely not showing *his* best side.

First they filled a big tub with

water for apple dunking.

Next they hung strings from
the rafters in the living room—
strings that would hold powdered
doughnuts.

Then they began blowing up
balloons.

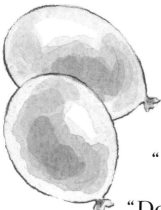

When Andy had blown

up thirteen balloons,

he got an idea.

"Let's set a trap!" he said.

"Don't be silly. What would

we need a trap for?"

asked Dolores.

"To trap the tricksters!"

exclaimed Andy. "I bet they'll

come back for your new pumpkin."

"They will?" asked Dolores.

"It's the best," said Andy. "You said it yourself."

Dolores thought for a moment. "I suppose we should figure out a trap," she said, picking up her clipboard and pen. "It's always good to plan ahead."

Andy couldn't believe his luck. Catching the tricksters was *his* idea of fun.

"Let's build a cage and hang it out
an upstairs window," he said. "Then
when the tricksters come up the
steps . . ."

Dolores stopped writing.

"We don't have any metal to build a cage with," she said.

Oh, thought Andy. *True enough.*

"We can dig a big hole," he said, "and cover it with sticks and leaves and grass and stuff. When the pumpkin smashers walk across the top, they'll fall in the pit and—"

"My father would *never* let us dig a hole in the yard," said Dolores. She crossed out the second idea.

"We can hang a bucket of water from a string," said Andy. "And when the tricksters are directly underneath—"

"How do you know that the tricksters will go *directly* underneath?" asked Dolores.

"All right, then," he said. "*You* think of an idea!"

"We'll be ghosts!" announced Dolores.

"Ghosts?" said Andy.

"Ghosts. And when the tricksters come up on the porch to steal the pumpkin, we'll rush out and scare them."

"No trap?" asked Andy.

"It *is* a trap," said Dolores. "It's just a different *kind* of trap."

Andy wasn't sure about her plan. But he didn't have a better one.

Andy and Dolores went to search

for sheets.

"You can wear this," said Dolores.

"It has flowers on it!" said Andy.

"My mom doesn't have any plain white sheets," said Dolores. "We can be the ghosts of the gardens—ghosts that scare anyone who messes with the glories of nature!"

"Oh, brother!" said Andy.

3

Not-So-Glorious Ghosts

Andy and Dolores huddled under the porch. It seemed as if they had been down there forever, waiting for it to get dark. Andy pulled a marble out of his pocket.

"Wow!" whispered Dolores. "I've never seen one that glows."

"This is my lucky marble," said Andy.

"May I hold it?" Dolores asked.

Just then Andy and Dolores heard
footsteps coming up the walkway.
Dolores peeked out from under the
steps and gave Andy the thumbs-up.
They pulled the sheets over their
heads.

"Ooooooh," Dolores moaned.

Andy followed her out from under the porch.

"Ooooooh," he groaned.

"What's that?" said one of the

tricksters.

"OOOOOOH!" Dolores yelled.

Andy couldn't see where he was going. He tripped on the hem of his sheet and fell face-down.

The tricksters doubled over laughing.

"Ooh, what scary ghosts!" one of them said.

Then they grabbed the pumpkin, smashed it on the ground, and took off running.

"Stop messing with our pumpkins!" Dolores shouted. "They're glories of nature!"

Andy untangled himself from his sheet.

What a stupid idea this was, he thought.

Then he saw Dolores kneeling over her smashed pumpkin. She was crying.

"Two pumpkins in two days," she sniffed.

That evening, Andy Shane pushed his meatballs from one side of his plate to the other.

"You look like I served you porcupine stew instead of your favorite supper," said Granny Webb.

"I still need to think of a present for Dolores," said Andy, carrying his plate over to the sink.

"Whoops!" he said.

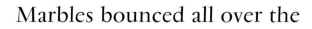

Marbles bounced all over the

kitchen floor.

Andy took a step and stumbled on a marble. And then another. His arms flailed in the air, but he couldn't keep his balance. He slip-slid to the floor.

"Aaugh!" he said. "This has been the worst day ever!"

"Have a nice *trip*? See you next *fall*!" Granny said, laughing. She was like that, always turning tragedy into fun.

Andy had to laugh, too. Then he started to collect all the marbles that had rolled from the kitchen counter to the front door.

That's when he got a great idea.

4

Tricking the Tricksters

Granny Webb carried the muffins
while Andy Shane carried the
roundest pumpkin to Dolores
Starbuckle's front door.

"Why, a spider and a fly have arrived!" Mrs. Starbuckle said.

"We're a *Grammostola rosea* and a *Musca domestica,*" said Granny Webb. She knew all the fancy names for bugs.

"Is that my present?" Dolores asked Andy.

Andy turned pink. "It's part of it," he said. "You have to wait for the rest."

"Come dunk for apples, then," said Dolores.

Andy followed Dolores to the tub

for apple dunking and to the strings

for doughnut munching.

Then Dolores took Andy to the haunted room to put his hands in a bowl full of eyeballs.

"Ugh," said Peter and Mindy.

"Mmmm," said Andy Shane, "*crunchy!*"

"How did you know they were grapes?" asked Dolores Starbuckle.

Andy just smiled. He didn't tell her that Granny Webb had played that trick on him last Halloween.

When the party was over, Andy

Shane and Granny Webb stayed to

help clean up.

Suddenly they heard a noise on

the porch.

"Shh!" said Andy. "It's the

tricksters."

"Well, I'm not going to let them

get my pumpkin again," said

Dolores.

"No, wait!" Andy said. "Watch."

Granny Webb came into the room and joined Andy and Dolores at the window. Andy felt like a soda-pop can that was about to burst.

One of the tricksters looked up and saw the three of them peering out. He grabbed the pumpkin and turned to run.

At that moment, the bottom of the pumpkin fell out.

Hundreds of marbles rolled down the porch steps.

Bimmety, Bimmety, Bim
BAM
Bim, BAM
Bim, bam

"Aaugh! Let's get out of here!" the

tricksters shouted.

"Andy Shane, you tricked the tricksters!" exclaimed Dolores.

She scooped the marbles into a plastic bag and handed it to him.

Andy smiled. He gave the bag back to Dolores.

"Happy birthday!" he said. "This is the second part of your present."

"Really?" said Dolores. "They're all for me?"

"Yup," said Andy. "That's half of
my collection. I kept the other half
so we could play marbles together."

"You'll play marbles with me?" asked Dolores.

Andy nodded.

"Tomorrow?"

"Sure," said Andy.

"This has turned out to be a great Halloween," Dolores said, "and a great birthday!"

Andy Shane had to agree.